Book 2 of the Sophie Series

Sophie and the Stream

Written by Pam Burgess

Illustrated by Aanu David

Sophie and the Stream
Book 2 of the Sophie Series
Copyright 2022 by Pam Burgess | pamburgess.com
Illustrated by Aanu David
Published by Argyle Fox Publishing | argylefoxpublishing.com
ISBN 978-1-953259-32-5 (Paperback)
ISBN 978-1-953259-31-8 (Hardcover)

It was bedtime, and Sophie had the wiggles.

"The fair is tomorrow!" she said, while slipping into her pajamas. "Annie and I have worked so hard on our scrumptious carrot muffins. Our friends will love them!"

She could almost taste the sweet nutty flavor of her prize muffins as she hopped into bed.

"Everyone will love your muffins," Sophie's mother said. "The sooner you fall asleep, the sooner the fair arrives."

"Then I need to go to sleep right away!" Sophie said.

Sophie's mother kissed her forehead and left Sophie to her dreams.

soph

Sophie snuggled in bed and clinched her eyes tight. She tried her best to fall asleep, but she was too excited.

"I can't sleep!" she said. "The fair will never get here if I stay awake."

Sophie threw the heavy blanket her mother made for her over her head. She hoped it would make the room so dark she couldn't help but fall asleep.

Through the heavy blanket, Sophie heard a faint scratching at the window. She peaked out to see Mr. Owliver glowing in the moonlight.

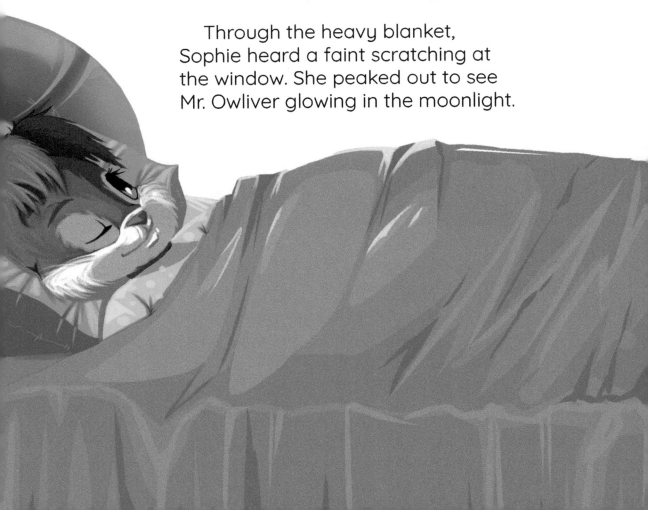

Sophie pushed the warm covers off, swung her feet over the side of her bed, and tiptoed to the window. She pushed on the window's wooden frame, opening the window enough for Mr. Owliver to lean in.

"Mr. Owliver," Sophie whispered, "it's very late!"

"Hellooo, Sophie," Mr. Owliver said. His voice was as loud and powerful as ever. He didn't seem to notice how late it was. "Tomorrooow is a big day, isn't it?"

"It is!" Sophie said excitedly. She covered her mouth, afraid her loud voice would wake her parents. "Tomorrow is the fair," she whispered. "Annie and I are taking our scrumptious carrot muffins!"

Mr. Owliver licked his beak.
"Just remember," he said, "yooou can chooose."

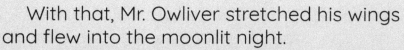

With that, Mr. Owliver stretched his wings and flew into the moonlit night.
Sophie closed the window, climbed back in bed, and pulled up the heavy blanket.

"What did Mr. Owliver mean?" she asked herself. Repeating Mr. Owliver's words in her head, Sophie's eyes grew heavy. Soon, she fell into a deep sleep.

Suddenly, Sophie was on an unfamiliar path surrounded by trees. Something in the nearby brush startled her. She turned to see a little brown squirrel who looked friendly. Sophie breathed a sigh of relief.

"Excuse me, sir," she said, "can you tell me if this is the way to the fair?"

The little squirrel stood on his hind legs for a better view of where Sophie was pointing.

"Yes," he finally squeaked, "it certainly is."

"Thank you!" Sofie said.

Sophie took off running. When she rounded the next bend, she stopped in her tracks. A broken pile of wood was in front of her. Sophie scratched her ear.

What is this? she wondered.

Then her heart sank. It wasn't a pile of wood. It was a bridge, broken into tiny pieces.

"Oh no!" Sophie said. "How could this happen to me?"

Sophie's shoulders slumped. She dropped to the ground and moped.

"I have such bad luck," she said. "This always happens to me!"

Just then, a breeze brushed Sophie's neck.
A whirl of feathers sounded overhead.

Sophie looked up. Mr. Owliver sat in the tree above her.

Sophie took a deep breath to hold back her tears.

"Hi, Mr. Owliver," she said softly.

"Yooou can chooose," Mr. Owliver hooted.

"What can I choose?" Sophie asked. Tears filled her eyes. "I don't understand," she said, her voice quivering.

Mr. Owliver alighted on the broken bridge.

"Yooou can chooose," he repeated before flying away.

Sophie wiped her eyes. Mr. Owliver was always nice, but—

"The bridge!" Sophie rose and stomped her foot. She knew what Mr. Owliver meant. "I'm going to the fair and this broken bridge is not going to stop me!"

She grabbed a piece of wood.
"I can use this wood to get across the stream!"

Sophie pulled and pulled. She pulled as hard as her little rabbit body could, but the wood didn't budge. She tugged harder, and the wood poked into her paw.
"Ouch!" she cried. "This is not fair—not fair at all!"

"Is something wrong?"
Sophie looked down. The little brown squirrel she met earlier leaned against a tree root.

"I need to use this wood to get across the stream," Sophie said, "but I can't move it."

"Oh," squeaked the squirrel, "that's too bad."

He shrugged his shoulders and disappeared into the woods. That gave Sophie an idea.

She stood up and brushed the leaves off of her clothes. Then followed the squirrel's path along the stream, deep into the woods.

Eventually, Sophie found a spot in the stream that was shallow and not very wide. The brush was thick near this spot, and it was not easy to walk. Thistles poked at Sophie's furry legs and arms. None of that slowed her down.

If I'm going to the fair, she thought, *I have to make a new way across the stream.*

Sophie ran to the edge of the woods and got to work. She removed brush and crushed thistles with her feet. Slowly, a new path came to life. However, something more was needed.

"Rocks!" Sophie said. "I need large stones to put in the stream so it will be easier to cross."

A pile of leaves jumped at the idea. Then the little brown squirrel ran out of the leaves, running from his chipmunk friend.

Sophie thought of her bright-eyed friend, Annie.

"Annie and I will have so much fun at the fair," Sophie mused. "But I need to make sure she can see this path!"

She walked to the opening of the trail. One after another, she laid stones in the shape of an arrow pointing the right direction.

When she finished the arrow, Sophie's back hurt. Making her new path was hard work, and there was more to do. She needed help.

"Excuse me, please," she called to the playing rodents. "Do you know anyone who could help me?"

The squirrel and chipmunk looked at each other.

"This new path might help us all," Sophie reasoned.

That idea got the rodents' attention.

"We could help!" squeaked the little brown squirrel.

"I think Zoë the deer could help too!" cried the chipmunk.

A few minutes later, Zoë came running toward Sophie and the squirrel. The chipmunk sat on Zoë's back, laughing.

"I'd be happy to help!" Zoë told Sophie. "I can help push the rocks into the stream."

The chipmunk slid off Zoë's back, and they all worked together. Soon, Sophie, Zoë, and the squirrel and chipmunk finished the path.

Sophie thanked everyone right before she slowly opened her eyes.

Sunlight filled her room. Sophie stretched and reflected on the dream that filled her night. Though she didn't know what today would bring, she knew Mr. Owliver was right.

"No matter what happens," Sophie said, "it's up to me what I do. I can choose!"

Sophie smiled and jumped out of bed, ready to take on whatever would come her way.

Mr. Owliver
ASKS

Do yooou sometimes feel bad when something stops you from doing what you want to dooo?

What do yooou think I meant by "Yooou can chooose."?

What might yooou do differently next time something doesn't go the way yooou wanted it to go?

How might others help yooou face obstacles?

How might yooou help yourself?

Get more at pamburgess.com.

About THE AUTHOR

   Pam Burgess lives with her husband on an inland lake in Michigan. She loves painting, photography, traveling, going to the movies and the theater, and playing with her grandchildren who live in Raleigh, North Carolina.

   Pam is a lifelong learner who enjoys discovering new insights and perspectives.

   In this book, Zoë the deer is named after Pam's second granddaughter (pictured right).

CPSIA information can be obtained
at www.ICGtesting.com
Printed in the USA
LVHW072355130922
728283LV00005B/83